D0229601

THE GREATEST ADVENTURES IN THE WORLD

ROBINSON CRUSOE

TONY BRADMAN & TONY ROSS

ORCHARD BOOKS

ORCHARD BOOKS
338 Euston Road, London NW1 3BH
Orchard Books Australia
Level 17/207 Kent Street, Sydney, NSW 2000
ISBN 978 1 40830 571 3 (hardback)
ISBN 978 1 40830 572 0 (paperback)
The text was first published in Great Britain in the form of a gift collection called *Heroes and Villains* with full colour illustrations by Tony Ross, in 2008
This edition first published in hardback in 2010
First paperback publication in 2011

A CIP catalogue record for this book is available from the British Library.
1 3 5 7 9 10 8 6 4 2 (hardback)
1 3 5 7 9 10 8 6 4 2 (paperback)
Printed & bound in the UK by J F Print Ltd., Sparkford, Somerset.
Orchard Books is a division of Hachette Children's Books,
an Hachette UK company.
www.hachette.co.uk

CONTENTS

CHAPTER ONE
ROBINSON CRUSOE 5

CHAPTER TWO
SHIPWRECKED! 11

CHAPTER THREE
DESERT ISLAND 23

CHAPTER FOUR
A HERO 35

NOTES ON THE STORY OF ROBINSON CRUSOE
BUILDING A HOME IN THE WILDERNESS 46

CHAPTER ONE

ROBINSON CRUSOE

YOUNG ROBINSON CRUSOE was a wild lad, the kind of boy who never did what he was told, and never listened to his father's advice. He thought his dad was just so…boring. Besides, what had Mr Crusoe Senior got to show for years of hard work and going without? A little money in the bank and a little house, that's what. Oh, and loads of daft sayings that he believed were the last word in wisdom. Stuff like "If a job's worth doing, Son, it's worth doing well" and "A place for everything, and everything in its place" and even "Where there's life, there's hope", for heaven's sake.

None of it made any sense to Robinson, and he spent a lot of time dreaming about a more exciting life, one of travel and adventure and riches. He also spent a lot of time trying to avoid the chores his father insisted on giving him. But Mr Crusoe was equally determined to make young Robinson do them. So as you can imagine, there were plenty of arguments in the Crusoe household.

Finally, Robinson could stand it no more and set off to seek his fortune. But he lived a topsy-turvy life, and he was never satisfied.

He certainly wasn't becoming wealthy as quickly as he had expected.

Then a chance came up for him to join a ship trading in the Caribbean. Robinson sold everything he owned and used the money to buy goods to sell. The ship left early one summer morning, the turquoise sea shimmering in the sunlight, and Robinson felt sure that his luck had changed.

It had, but only for the worse. On the second day of the voyage, a wild hurricane blew, and the howling winds quickly drove the ship so far off-course that the captain had no idea where they were. Robinson felt horribly sick, and grimly held onto a mast.

Suddenly there was a CRASH! and the ship juddered to a halt, its masts swaying.

"We've struck a reef!" yelled the captain at last. "We're stuck on it too, and the sea will soon smash the hull to pieces… ABANDON SHIP!"

CHAPTER TWO

SHIPWRECKED!

THE CREW WRESTLED THE lifeboat into the sea, and they all jumped in. But in no time at all, a giant wave had swamped them. Robinson fell into the foaming sea and felt himself

being sucked down. He held his breath till he thought his lungs would burst. Then he was driven back to the surface, and the sea dumped him on a beach. Robinson turned round and saw another giant wave heading straight for him…

Three times the terrible sea caught him, even though he tried his best to outrun it, and three times it swallowed him and spat him out, but always further and further up the beach.

At last it left him alone, and he crawled painfully into the shelter of some palm trees. Behind the palms there was jungle too thick for the moonlight to penetrate. Maybe it was full of savage beasts? Robinson felt his heart pounding, and tried to sleep.

He woke to the sounds of the sea sighing and birds squawking. The storm was over but Robinson couldn't see the reef itself because of the morning mist rolling in over it from the sea beyond.

He stood there for a moment, wondering what had happened to his shipmates. Then he caught sight of an object lying half-buried in the sand nearby. It was the captain's hat. He soon found another hat, and then a couple of shoes that didn't match. But otherwise the beach was empty, and he began to realise that he might be the only survivor.

Feeling desolate, Robinson sat down heavily and covered his face with his hands. After a while he looked up again and noticed the mist clearing. There was a shadow on the reef, and as the light grew stronger, Robinson saw something that gave him hope – the ship! Maybe some of the crew had made it back to the ship after the lifeboat had been overturned. There was only one way to find out.

Robinson swam out across the lagoon. The water was warm and soothing, and it didn't take him too long to reach the reef.

He found a rope dangling from the bows, and used it to haul himself aboard.

"Ahoy, shipmates!" he called out. "Is there anyone there?"

But there was no reply.

Robinson went below decks to search the cabins and heard a strange noise coming from inside one. He pulled the door open, and three small shapes dashed out between his feet, knocking him down.

For a brief instant Robinson panicked.

Then he felt a large, wet tongue scraping at his face, and a pair of soft, small heads nuzzling against him. It was Toby, the captain's dog, and the ship's cats, a young, white female called Freckles, and an old ginger tom called Rufus.

"All right, Toby," said Robinson, laughing and trying to push the dog down. “You can stop licking me now. Boy, am I pleased to see you!”

Robinson returned to the top deck, the animals following him.

He leaned against the main mast and looked back at the island.

A steep, rocky hill rose up within the dense jungle. He realised now that the island was quite small, its geography clear in the bright morning sun.

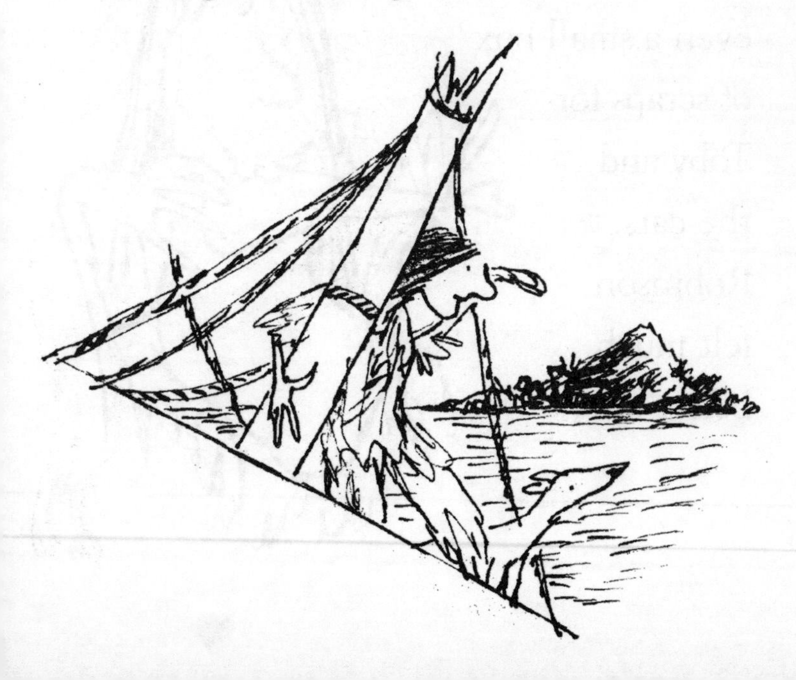

There was no sign of human habitation anywhere.

"So, Toby, my old messmate," Robinson murmured, "it seems we're in a pretty lonely spot. What do you think I should do?" He glanced down at the dog. "No ideas? Can't say I'm surprised. Still, shall we see what we can find?"

There were plenty of supplies in the galley, even a small box of scraps for Toby and the cats. Robinson felt much better after a hearty meal, and ready to come up with a plan of action.

He wasn't sure, but he thought the island wasn't near the main trading routes, so it could be a long time before another ship found him. He would have to survive until then, so it was a tremendous stroke of luck that the ship hadn't sunk. The food would keep him going while he worked out what the island had to offer. And of course there were other things to be had on such a vessel – ropes and timber and canvas, tools and nails for starters.

"In fact, there's just about everything I need, Toby," Robinson said. "But I'm sure the ship will sink tonight, so I need to get as much as possible from it." He looked around the deck, noticed some spars that had fallen from a mast – and had an idea. "I know...I'll make a raft!"

CHAPTER THREE

DESERT ISLAND

ROBINSON LASHED THE SPARS and pieces of timber together with ropes from the rigging, and before long his raft was bobbing on the sea. He loaded it with as much as he could and soon he was ready to leave. Freckles and Rufus jumped down to join him.

"Come on, Toby!" laughed Robinson, preparing to shove off with a pole he'd made. "You'll be safe, I promise!"

Toby whined, then leapt into the sea with a huge SPLASH! Robinson tried to get him to climb onto the raft, but Toby didn't want to, and swam beside it all the way to the shore.

Robinson dragged the raft up the beach and unloaded his stores beyond the high water mark.

"Right," said Robinson. "Time to do some exploring."

Robinson, Toby and the cats walked along the beach until they came to a stream that emerged from the jungle and flowed into the sea.

"Ah, fresh water," said Robinson, smiling. "That's good…"

The stream twisted and turned through the jungle and finally led to the rocky hill Robinson had seen from the ship. At the base of the hill was a clearing and the entrance to a small cave. The perfect place to build his shelter.

Within a few hours he had taken all his stores to the cave, and used a spare sail to make an awning in front of it. He chopped down a couple of trees for firewood, sharpened the branches into stakes, and planted them in a semi-circle round the edge of the clearing as a fence. It took him all afternoon, but it certainly made him feel a lot safer.

He lit a fire and sat beside it to eat his supper with Toby dozing next to him. Freckles and Rufus had found them, and lay cuddled up to each other and the dog.

Robinson dozed off himself as the sun went down, although he didn't sleep well, his dreams full of winds and waves and fierce wild animals.

He woke early the next morning, his spirits low, but at least the ship was still there, perched on the reef.

Robinson lost count of the number of trips he made from shore to ship and ship to shore, then back up the beach and through the jungle to his cave. It was hard work in the hot sun, but it gave him huge satisfaction to see his heap of supplies growing. He only stopped when the sun went down.

"Phew, what a day!" he said as he ate his evening meal. "But it was definitely worth it. If nothing else, at least we've got some light now!"

Robinson had found a dozen candles in the captain's cabin, and now one lit the inside of his cave with a cosy golden glow. He was beginning to feel relaxed for the first time since the shipwreck. And when he slept that night, he dreamed only of what he was going to do with his stores.

The next day, Robinson discovered to his delight that the ship still hadn't sunk. That gave him the chance to make more trips on the raft to it, and to bring away more stuff that might be useful. The ship was there the next day, and the day after that, and the day after, and Robinson slipped into a busy routine of trips to the ship and work on his shelter.

He spent part of each day sorting his booty and storing it away properly in the cave. And in between doing all that, he and Toby explored as much of the island as possible.

"I think we're going to be fine, Toby," Robinson said as they were heading home late one afternoon. It was the twelfth day since the wreck. "It's not such a scary place as I thought. There aren't any dangerous wild animals here, just lots of goats, and I can hunt them for meat. I might even be able to catch a few and keep them for their milk. And there are fish in the lagoon, so Freckles and Rufus can have the occasional treat."

That evening, Robinson sat in his cave surrounded by his supplies in their neat piles. He frowned, a memory nagging somewhere at the back of his mind. And then it came to him, and he found himself thinking about his father.

"A place for everything, and everything in its place," Robinson said, and smiled.

"I think Dad would be impressed, Toby," he said. "And what was that other thing he used to say? Oh yes, 'If a job's worth doing, it's worth doing well.' Do you know, I can see the point of that now. I've done a pretty good job of stripping the ship of anything that might be useful, but there's still plenty aboard. So I'll keep going until the job is done."

Robinson lay down, his head full of plans, and quickly fell asleep. He didn't sleep for long, though. That night there was a great storm. Robinson huddled in his cave with Toby and Freckles and Rufus, all of them jumping when the thunder went…BOOM!

CHAPTER FOUR

A HERO

THE STORM ENDED AT DAWN, and Robinson set off with Toby to see what it had done to the island. The jungle looked rather battered, and lots of broken branches were strewn across the beach.

As Robinson walked along, he remembered that this was his thirteenth day as a castaway.

Then he looked out to the reef, and saw that the ship had vanished.

Robinson's heart sank, and the good mood and confidence of the last few days crumbled.

He turned around and walked away, his head down, stumbling into the jungle.

Then he started running, Toby barking at his heels. Robinson ran and ran and ran, crashing through the branches and undergrowth, and after a while he realised he was heading upwards, the ground rising beneath his feet. Soon he found himself at the top of the rocky hill.

From there he could have seen the whole island, the dark blue sea surrounding it calm and flat again now after the storm. But his eyes were full of tears, and for a time he could see nothing. He felt Toby gently nudge his leg, and the dog whined, confused and worried about his master.

Robinson realised that the ship was more than a source of supplies. In his mind it had been a link with the outside world, a talisman, proof somehow that one day another ship would come along and rescue him. Now he felt more alone than he had ever done before.

What point was there in everything he'd done since the shipwreck? There was probably nothing ahead of him but years of solitude and hardship and struggle, and finally a sad, lonely death. He might as well save himself the bother and simply jump off the nearest cliff.

There was a steep drop in front of him, and he moved towards it. He closed his eyes, felt the wind tug at him – and suddenly he remembered something else his father used to say.

It was almost as if he could hear his father's voice speaking inside his head. "Where there's life, there's hope..."

"You were right, Dad," Robinson murmured, suddenly understanding. He opened his eyes, looked down at Toby, and fondled the dog's ears. "For all we know, Toby, a ship might turn up tomorrow," he said. "And if I'm dead, I won't be here to greet it, will I?

"No, I'm alive, and I think I'd like to stay that way. Come on, let's go home. I've still got chores to do. Hey, did I say chores?" he laughed. "If only Dad could see me now!" Robinson strode off, Toby running along beside him, happy to see his master smiling again.

There was no ship the next day, or the day after that, or the day after that. In fact, it was many years before Robinson was rescued, and there were many more dark moments before that day. But Robinson never, ever gave up hope, and that's what made him a hero.

Not the kind of hero who does daring deeds and has great adventures seeking glory, of course. Robinson Crusoe was a quiet hero, a bit like his father – a man who took what life dealt him, and did the best he could.

And sometimes that's just about the hardest kind of hero to be.

ROBINSON CRUSOE

Building a Home in the Wilderness

By Tony Bradman

Robinson Crusoe is a very famous book. It has been translated into dozens of languages, and has been turned into plays, TV programmes and films – there was even one film called *Robinson Crusoe In Space*! So what is it about this story of a man marooned on a desert island that has made it so popular?

The book's author, Daniel Defoe, was born in London in 1660, and led an exciting and varied life. At different times he was a soldier, a merchant, a sea-farer and a spy. But for most of his life he was also a writer. He wrote over 500 books covering a vast range of subjects – politics, travel, crime, religion.

Then one day, when he was already nearly 60, he came across a book about a certain Alexander Selkirk, a sailor who had been marooned on a desert island for four years. This true story must have captured Daniel's imagination, for soon he wrote *Robinson Crusoe*, a made-up tale of adventure and survival.

Daniel's book was published in 1719, and was an immediate success. One reason was that in those days before cars and aeroplanes, few people travelled more than a few miles from where they lived. So a story set in the faraway Caribbean was fascinating – it was almost like reading about a trip to Mars!

People have always loved stories about visits to exotic lands, like the voyage of Jason and his Argonauts in search of The Golden Fleece. But it's the theme of survival that gives *Robinson Crusoe* its greatest appeal. Everyone who reads it asks the same question – would I be able to survive in the same situation?

The shipwrecked Robinson manages to build a home in the wilderness and create a life for himself. Of course he's lucky enough to have all the useful stuff he salvages from the wreck. But he's still incredibly resourceful and inventive, and he's brave, too, in dealing with all sorts of problems, including loneliness. Last but not least, his story has a happy ending – which is always good!

ORCHARD MYTHS AND CLASSICS

TONY BRADMAN & TONY ROSS

Jason and the Voyage to the Edge of the World	978 1 84362 466 0
Arthur and the King's Sword	978 1 84362 470 7
Aladdin and the Fabulous Genie	978 1 84362 471 4
Ali Baba and the Stolen Treasure	978 1 84362 467 7
Robin Hood and the Silver Arrow	978 1 84362 468 4
William Tell and the Apple for Freedom	978 1 84362 469 1
Robinson Crusoe, Shipwrecked	978 1 84362 571 3
Beowulf the Hero	978 1 84362 573 7
Gulliver in Lilliput	978 1 84362 575 1
David and Goliath	978 1 84362 577 5

All priced at £8.99